The Little
Van Gogh
in Provence

Catherine de Duve

Have fun discovering Van Gogh's Provence!

KATE'ART
EDITIONS

South of France

Vincent van Gogh arrives in Arles by train in February 1888. The painter has just spent two years with his brother Theo in Paris, and now needs sunshine and colors! But it's still winter and it's cold. What does he find?

Saint-Trophime Cathedral

Place de la République

Vincent van Gogh
Arles

SCOOP

Arles was nicknamed the "Little Rome of Gaul". It has the biggest arena – amphitheatre – in France.

Arles

When he arrives, Van Gogh rents a room at Hotel-Restaurant Carrel. From there he sets out to discover the town.
"What beautiful women there are in Arles!", he thinks.

He visits the Roman theatre, the thermal baths, the arena, the museums and the churches. Vincent buys some paints and gets down to work. There's no time to lose!

Arena

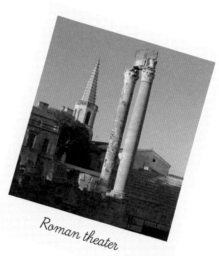

Roman theater

Réattu Museum

3

Yellow house

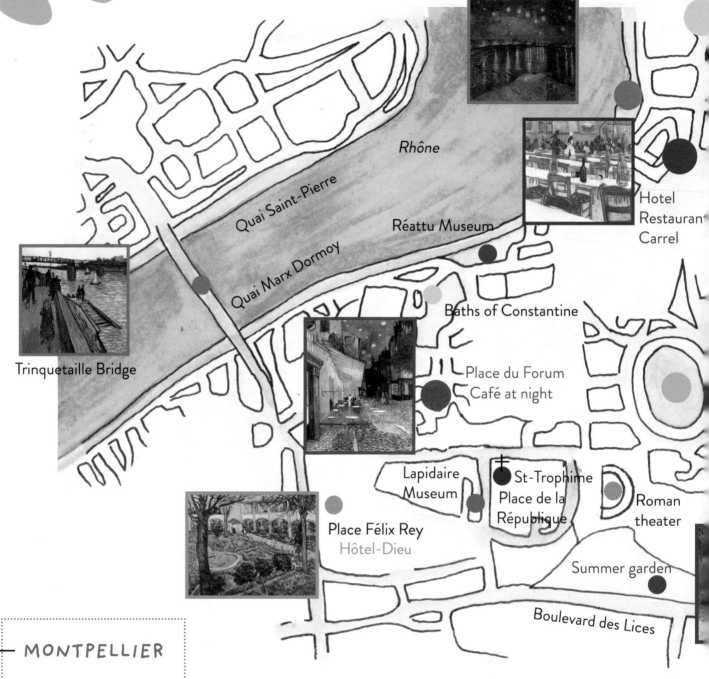

Rhône

Quai Saint-Pierre

Quai Marx Dormoy

Réattu Museum

Hotel Restaurant Carrel

Trinquetaille Bridge

Baths of Constantine

Place du Forum Café at night

Lapidaire Museum

St-Trophime
Place de la République

Roman theater

Place Félix Rey
Hôtel-Dieu

Summer garden

Boulevard des Lices

← MONTPELLIER

VAN-GOGH BRIDGE ▶

Station café

Place martine

SAINT-RÉMY-DE-PROVENCE
FONTVIEILLE
ABBAYE DE MONTMAJOUR

Rue de la Roubine du Roy

e Arena

Chemin de Fer

Roubine du Roy

Rue Mireille

Old Windmill

In the footsteps of van Gogh in Arles

Avenue Victor Hugo

Alyscamps

SAINTES-MARIES-
DE-LA-MER

The Yellow House

The "Colorists"

Van Gogh rents a room above the station café, Place Lamartine, 100 meters from the river Rhône. Here he also finds a little yellow house. Nobody has lived in it for some time, it's not too expensive and he can rent it, set up his own studio there and store his many paintings.

Vincent's dream is to create a house for artists where they can all work together. They would call themselves the "Colorists"!

The yellow house

SCOOP

The yellow house was destroyed in the bombings in 1944.

Vincent's bedroom

On the first floor, Vincent makes a
comfortable bedroom for himself.
He wants to feel at home and buys
some furniture. Everything is very tidy!
Usually, though, Vincent is very untidy...

Vincent's bedroom

Vincent's friends

Vincent makes new friends in Provence. Here are Roulin **the postman,** Milliet the **second lieutenant of a Zouave regimen**t, and the painter and **poet** Eugène Boch. He paints their portraits.

Roulin

Milliet

Boch

Van Gogh's Café

Van Gogh's Café nowadays!

Nature is waking up. The fruit trees are in blossom... Vincent hurries to paint the trees in the orchards, as the Southern wind will soon blow off the petals. What a wonderful sight! "It's so beautiful!", he thinks. Vincent is happy.

SCOOP
When the wind is too strong, Vincent has to tie down his easel, or puts his canvas on his knees so it doesn't blow away. Vincent paints very quickly!

Allée des Pins
Fontvieille

Windmill

The month of May is here. Van Gogh goes to visit a friend's studio in Fontvieille. On the way there he draws the landscapes, fields and windmills, which remind him of his homeland. Does he meet the French writer **Alphonse Daudet** there?

Daudet's windmill

 # camargue

It'll soon be June, and it's getting hotter and hotter. Van Gogh travels to the sea. "I wonder what the Mediterranean looks like?", he thinks to himself. He crosses the country in a stagecoach. What can he see? The Camargue region, with its "mas" (farmhouses), reeds, flamingos, marshes and white horses... Soon, in the distance, he sees the church tower of Saintes-Maries.

Camargue

Lavender

Here, nature is extraordinarily beautiful!

Mediterranean

Sea, sun, sand

Vincent spends a few days in this fishermen's village.
He draws the huts and boats. He paints oil seascapes
and watches the changing colors of the sea.
At night he walks alone on the deserted beach.

Fishermen's village

Gypsies

Summer

A gypsy family have set up camp not far from Vaccarès lake. It's very hot this August. The children go off exploring while the horses graze on the scorched grass around the caravans. Van Gogh painted them.

The fairground people

Sunflowers

Sunflowers

The fields of sunflowers at the roadside smile at Vincent. Like him, they're looking for the sun. He paints many pictures of them, as he wants to surprise the painter Paul Gauguin who's arriving soon. Vincent is waiting for him and is decorating his house with sunflowers. What a lovely welcome!

Bridges

Vincent paints the metal bridge at Trinquetaille, which spans the river Rhône. How modern! On the canals around Arles, Vincent finds the pretty drawbridges. The washerwomen chat while washing their clothes and linen in the river. These bridges were built by a Dutch engineer, and remind him of the Netherlands, but also of Japan!

Trinquetaille Bridge, Arles

Montmajour

Abbey of Montmajour

Sunset

The crickets are singing on the *"Plaine de la Crau"*. Heat is rising in the grove of oak trees at the foot of **Montmajour Abbey**. The air is scented with thyme and rosemary. Van Gogh admires the bright yellows of the sunset.

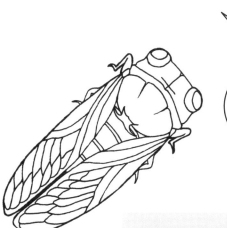

I work in the heat of the day, in full sunlight, like a cricket!

"Plaine de la Crau"

Van Gogh's bridge

SCOOP
Langlois bridge was named after the man who used to work there, but is now known as Van-Gogh Bridge. Vincent paints it 11 times.

AlysCamps

The Alyscamps

Rows of sarcophagi

Autumn

It's already autumn! Gauguin arrives at last.
For two months, the artists leave home early
in the morning to paint the surrounding area,
the Alyscamps, and its rows of **Roman sarcophagi**
and the banks of the Rhône, right beside their
house. They also go to Montpellier and visit the
Fabre Museum.

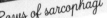
Madame Ginoux

Portrait

When it rains, Madame Ginoux,
the landlady of the station
café, poses for the two artists.
She is dressed in typical Arles
costume. Van Gogh paints
her very quickly, in just one
session, against a bright yellow
background!

Hôtel-Dieu

Van Gogh & Gauguin

It's Christmas Eve. The two painters often quarrel and Paul Gauguin wants to leave. Desperately upset, Van Gogh cuts off his own ear-lobe.
He is completely beside himself and passes out.
He goes to **Hôtel-Dieu hospital** to be treated.
Gauguin returns to Paris. Soon Vincent feels a little better and paints the cloisters and his garden.

Self-portrait

The cloister then

The cloister now

Saint-Rémy

A quiet place

Vincent is tired. He's looking for a quiet place where he can rest. On 8th May 1889 he arrives at **Saint-Paul-de-Mausole asylum**, a former medieval convent. But as Vincent often has fits, the doctor will not allow him to go out. Fortunately, Van Gogh has two rooms, one to sleep in and the other to paint in. What can he see through the bars on his window? The painter sits in the cloisters and garden and admires the flowers.

When Vincent paints, he forgets all his troubles!

Saint-Paul-de-Mausole

View from Saint-Rémy-de-Provence

SCOOP
Vincent paints 140 pictures in Saint-Rémy alone!

I have so many ideas for my work!

Mountains

In June, Vincent is at last allowed out! He paints pictures of the Alpilles mountains, of the fields, wild irises, olive groves... But, oh no!

The painter has another crisis and swallows some paint. Poor Van Gogh is very unhappy.

The Alpilles mountains

*"I often think that
the night-time is even more
colourful than the daytime".*

What a night!

Vincent's mind is full of the
landscapes of Provence.
He paints using small semi-
circular brush-strokes.
The lines snake across the
picture, the church tower
casts a mysterious shadow,
the cypress trees seem to
be on fire.... It's night-time
in Vincent's mind. But the
stars and the moon are
shining like diamonds in
the night! In the painter's
hands, they take on all sorts
of colors: yellows, greens,
pinks... How beautiful!

Text: Catherine de Duve

Concept and production: Kate'Art Editions

Translation: Rachel Cowler

Photographic credits:

Vincent van Gogh

Amsterdam: Van Gogh Museum: *Self-portrait as a painter*, 1888: cover p.1 - *Vincent's house in Arles (The Yellow House)*, 1888: pp.4-6 – *Vincent's bedroom in Arles*, 1888: p.7 – *Fishing boats on the beach at Saintes-Maries-de-la-mer*, 1888: p.13 – *Sunflowers*, 1888: p.15 – *Sunset at Montmajour*, 1888: p.17.

Londres: Courtauld Institute Gallery: *Self-portrait with Bandaged Ear*, 1889: p.19.

Otterlo: Kröller-Müller Museum: *Terrace of a café at night (Place du Forum)*, 1888: p.4, p.8 – *Portrait of Milliet, Second Lieutenant of the Zouaves*, 1888: p.8 – *View of Saintes-Maries*, 1888: p.12 – *Trinquetaille bridge in Arles*, 1888: p.4, p.16 – *Langlois bridge at Arles with women washing*, 1888: p.4, p.17 – *The Alyscamps, falling autumn leaves*, 1888: p.5, p.18 – *La Roubine du Roy*, 1888: p.5.

Paris: Orsay Museum: *Portrait of Eugene Boch*, 1888: p.8 – *The Caravans, gypsy camp near Arles*, 1888: p.14 – *Starry night over the Rhône*, 1888: p.4.

Winterthur: Oskar Reinhart Collection: *The courtyard of the hospital at Arles*, 1889: p.4, p.19.

St-Petersburg: Hermitage Museum: *Spectators in the arena at Arles*, 1888: p.5.

Sao Paulo: Museu de Arte de Sao Paulo: *L'Arlésienne (Madame Ginoux)*, 1890: p.18.

USA: New York: Museum of Modern Art: *Olive Trees with the Alpilles in the background*, 1889: p.21 – *The Starry Night*, 1889: p.22. **Boston: Museum of Fine Arts:** *Portrait of the Postman Joseph Roulin*, 1888: p.8. **Buffalo: Albright-Knox Art Gallery:** *The Old Mill*, 1888: p.5. **Washington: Phillips Collection:** *Entrance to the public park in Arles*, 1888: p.5. **New Haven: Yale University Art Gallery:** *Night Café in the Place Lamartine in Arles*, 1888: p.5.

Zürich: Kunsthaus Zürich: *Three White Cottages in Saintes-Maries*, 1888: p.13.

Private collection: *View from Vincent's bedroom, Saint-Rémy-de-Provence*, 1889: p.20 - *Interior of the Restaurant Carrel in Arles*, 1888: p.4.

Photographs: Private collection: pp.2-3, p.8, pp.10-11, pp.16-21.

With thanks to everone involved in the production of this book.

Did you like this book?

Vincent **Van Gogh**

The Little **Van Gogh in Provence**

The Impressionists' from Monet to Van Gogh **JAPAN**

Visit our online shop

www.kateart.com